Sir Anthony and the Star Stone Crystal

Greg Way

AuthorHouse™
1663 Liberty Drive
Bloomington, IN 47403
www.authorhouse.com
Phone: 833-262-8899

Because of the dynamic nature of the Internet, any web addresses or links contained in this book may have changed since publication and may no longer be valid. The views expressed in this work are solely those of the author and do not necessarily reflect the views of the publisher, and the publisher hereby disclaims any responsibility for them.

Any people depicted in stock imagery provided by Getty Images are models, and such images are being used for illustrative purposes only.
Certain stock imagery © Getty Images.

This book is printed on acid-free paper.

ISBN: 978-1-4389-6255-9 (sc)

Library of Congress Control Number: 2009907379

Print information available on the last page.

Published by AuthorHouse 04/18/2024

authorHOUSE

Preface

Once upon a time long ago in a land far away, when darkness stilled the air, there lived a man whose name was Yoriah. He was a humble man. Some say he lived all alone, far beyond the hills, high up in the mountains where only eagles were said to fly. It is also said that this man was a man of great magic and wisdom a man who could turn wishes into reality and stones into gold but his own loneliness he could not cure. One day he was out fetching water at a nearby stream when he heard a thunderous sound in the sky. He looked up into the sky and was amazed to see a star shooting down from the heavens. As he watched this star descend from the sky, Yoriah saw that the star was headed right toward him, so out of fear he ran for safety and ducked for cover behind some rocks that lay close by. Then he looked up just as the star came crashing down into the stream from where he was fetching water. In curiosity Yoriah went to where the star had landed. He picked it up, and immediately Yoriah was given power from this star to speak to all the animals of the land. In fact, Yoriah could also hear and understand what the animals were saying; and from then on the magic man, Yoriah, found that he would never be lonely again. For the star that fell from the sky was not an ordinary star at all; it was the Star Stone Crystal, and it is said that whoever shall possess this Star Crystal will be given from it the power to make right all that is wrong. It is also said that to gain all the Star Crystal's power one must first be of pure heart and of royalty to use its power to defeat the evil dragons of Nomans Land and destroy the Lord of Shadows forever.

And so comes the story of Sir Anthony and the Star Stone Crystal.

Enjoy the journey.

Special thanks to my good friend Ray who was so helpful in the process of completing this book.
To all my awesome friends so many miles away—David, Allyssa, Charlotte, Richard, Alicia, and Tina: dreams do come true after all!

Back in the days of chivalry and shining armor when good triumphed over evil, kings and queens fought to protect their children and townspeople from evil dragons that would pillage and destroy cities. It was in these days that there lived a young warrior named Sir Anthony. He was the son of the royal Princess Patricia and Prince Gregory.

Sir Anthony was a young warrior who fought with honor. He was also heir to the throne of the city of Goodinia, where he lived.

Chapter 1

Part 1

The Battle

All was quiet in the city of Goodinia. The year was 513 AD. In the fall of that year, the nights were as cool as the days were long, and it was on a cool and peaceful night such as this that the city streets and the markets were filled with people shopping for food and exchanging the town's latest gossip. There was joy and laughter everywhere with children in the town square skipping rope and playing happily together. Then suddenly, out of nowhere and without any warning, from out of the sky came a dragon flying toward the city with its monstrous wings spread wide, breathing fire down on the town's markets and homes with its talons and claws wreaking terror on the city and its townspeople.

And at once the king and queen put out the order for their best warriors to fight the evil dragon's rampage; among these warriors were Prince Gregory and Sir Anthony, the best and mightiest warriors the king and queen had. The battle was on. Sir Anthony and Prince Gregory had managed to back the dragon out of their city with sword and scimitar in hand. The two warriors fought bravely, and just as Prince Gregory was about to land the final striking blow that would kill the evil dragon and rid it from the city, the beastly dragon with eyes of fire spread its wings and took to the air. When it came down again it stretched out its mighty claws and with sharp talons grabbed hold of Prince Gregory. In the strike he dropped his sword to the ground below. Just as the dragon was making its escape back into Nomans Land, Sir Anthony cried out in a loud voice, saying, "Take heart, Father. Do not despair. For I, Sir Anthony, shall come quickly to save you." And then the dragon with Prince Gregory in its clutches was out of sight beyond the mountains, heading toward its lair in Nomans Land. Sir Anthony, with a tear-struck face, picked up his father's sword, mounted his horse, and then sped at breakneck speed back to the castle to tell his mother, Princess Patricia, what had happened.

The news of what had happened made the princess very sad, for she knew about Nomans Land. She loved Prince Gregory with all her heart, and she knew that Nomans Land was ruled by the evil dragons and that no man ever went there because of the chance that he might never return home. But even though Sir Anthony was the son of the prince and princess and heir to the throne of Goodinia, he was also the best warrior and swords-man in all the land and the best and only chance Prince Gregory had of making it back alive.

Now the dragon that took Prince Gregory away made Sir Anthony very angry, so angry that Sir Anthony made a vow to his mother that he would go and save his father and kill the evil dragon that stole him away. With the heart of a lion, Sir Anthony was unstoppable, for he was indeed a mighty warrior, the best in all the land of Goodinia, and he had the love of his mother and father to strengthen him. But Sir Anthony knew that saving his father would not be an easy task, for the journey to Nomans Land was a long and dangerous one, and once there he would be fighting against the dragon's prime evil, which he had never known before.

The very next morning Sir Anthony prepared for his journey to Nomans Land. He took with him all the weapons he would need to fight the beasts of the forests, and he took along all the food and water he would need for himself and his horse, because the journey, he knew, would be a long and quite exhausting one, and he would need these things to keep safe and well for the battle ahead. But before he departed Goodinia, his mother, Princess Patricia, gave to him charms so that they might charm the spirits of the forest, and she also gave to Sir Anthony a very ancient map that would lead him to the magical man Yoriah, who lived at the mountain's peak high above the clouds. With a warm embrace and a kiss from his mother, Sir Anthony was off and on his way to save his father, Prince Gregory, from the evil dragons of Nomans Land.

Princess Patricia wept silent tears of sadness and joy as her beloved son, Sir Anthony, sped across the great plains of Goodinia, and like the wind, Sir Anthony was out of sight. All the while Princess Patricia prayed that no harm would come to her son and that he would find his father and bring him back to her unharmed from the clutches of the evil dragons. And so it was by nightfall that Sir Anthony reached the foothills of the great mountain where the magical man, Yoriah, was said to live. The forest that lay between was no place to be in at night, for in it many fierce and dangerous beasts prowled the floor. But since the young warrior, Sir Anthony, was heavily armed with his weapons and the charms that his mother had given him, he was not in the least bit frightened by the many beasts that awaited. With a kick to the flank of his horse, Sir Anthony was on his way and into the dark and heavily wooded forest. Although it was night, the moon was full and shining at its brightest, which made it possible for Sir Anthony to see fairly well so that he could stay clear from danger as best he could for him and his horse.

Hours had passed since he started at the forest's edge. Along the way he had passed many great oak trees and many exotic birds and creatures of all sorts. Sir Anthony wondered how many more strange creatures he might just encounter along the way. Just then out of nowhere leaped a very large and fierce beast, and with its massive jaws open wide and its long sharp teeth sticking out it was about to pounce on Sir Anthony. But the young warrior was lightning quick, and in just the blink of an eye Sir Anthony drew his sword and pierced the deadly beast. As the beast was falling to the ground the young warrior drew his bow, pulled back on his arrow, and then let it fly, striking the fatal blow and killing the beast. Then looking around to make sure of no more danger and seeing no danger near, Sir Anthony was once again on his way to the mountain peak that waited above the clouds.

Once through the forest and about halfway up the mountain's pass, Sir Anthony stopped his horse at a nearby stream to rest awhile, and just then, out of the sky, more terror came. It was a giant bird of prey, tearing out of the sky with its claws stretched wide, waiting to tear at the horse's throat. The bird, screeching like a banshee—the sound of a wild witch—bore down now upon the horse. Sir Anthony without hesitation took hold of the charm his mother had given him and, holding the charm to his heart, cried out in a loud voice, "By the power of good: evil be gone!" At once the beastly bird was gone and Sir Anthony and his horse were safe once again, and he silently thanked his mother for giving him the charm that saved his life. Without wasting any more time Sir Anthony forged on with his journey. At about midway up the mountain he came upon a path, and he looked, and there along the path grew the most beautiful flowers of all colors. They reminded him of his mother, Princess Patricia, for she had the most beautiful flowers, and she placed them all around the castle, inside and out. The flowers also reminded him of his mother and the beauty she possessed, her hair, the fairest in the land, golden blond hair that seemed to flow in the wind. To Sir Anthony, Princess Patricia was the most beautiful in all the land of Goodinia, and he shared these thoughts with his father, Prince Gregory.

Sir Anthony, mighty and brave as he was, could not stand the thought of his mother having to live without his father by her side. And as a single tear flowed down the young warrior's cheek, he vowed once again that he would free his father from the evil dragon and then kill the fire-breathing beast of Nomans Land and put an end to any further attacks on the city of Goodinia. With this thought in mind, Sir Anthony once again pressed on with his journey until he came upon the end of the path where the flowers stopped and the clouds began.

As Sir Anthony looked up into the clouds he could see no further, and not knowing what lay beyond the clouds he wondered what creatures he might encounter once through. But then, all of a sudden, through the stillness around him he heard something or someone call his name. Not knowing what to expect he took hold once again of the charm his mother gave him, and just then he heard his name called again, and he looked up to the clouds. Then, out of the clouds, came an eagle calling to Sir Anthony and saying, "Do not fear me, for I am a messenger of Yoriah, the one whom you seek. I have been sent by him to show you the way to his castle with a message for you, Sir Anthony."

And with that, Sir Anthony put away his charm for he felt no battle with this eagle. Then the eagle said to the young warrior, "Come. I will take you to Yoriah. He wishes to help you in your quest to save your father from the evil dragons of Nomans Land."

Sir Anthony was amazed, for he had never seen nor heard of an eagle with the ability of speech. So he followed the creature and was led through the clouds, and once through he looked and saw the most beautiful rainbow he had ever seen. It seemed to stretch from one side of the mountain to the other, and underneath the rainbow was a waterfall that fed a stream that flowed alongside a magnificent castle that no doubt belonged to the magical man, Yoriah. Everywhere all around Sir Anthony gathered animals of all kind—deer, rabbits, birds, squirrels, and even bears—and they were all gentle in nature and welcomed Sir Anthony to their land.

Sir Anthony was amazed at all the wonders he saw in this land, and he wondered what magic they came from, and then the eagle said to Sir Anthony, "Take heart, young warrior, for just as Yoriah has given speech to all you see here, he shall also help you in your journey to save your father." And then the eagle flew off into the sky and rested on top of the rainbow above the waterfall. Then the magic man, Yoriah, came out of his castle to greet Sir Anthony.

"Welcome to my land," said Yoriah to the young warrior. "I have been expecting you. Come, let us enter my castle, for you have had a long journey, and you must be hungry and thirsty. I shall give you food and drink and a place for you to rest. Later we shall get started on your quest to free your father from Nomans Land."

"Thank you, kind sir," said Sir Anthony, "for your gracious hospitality."

"My boy, you are more than welcome," said Yoriah. "I am a friend to the king and queen of Goodinia. How do you think you came to have a map showing you the way to my kingdom?" Then the ancient Yoriah gave a hearty chuckle, and said, "Come, let us eat and drink, for in the morning a long journey awaits you, young warrior."

So Yoriah and Sir Anthony ate supper and had tea to drink, and later on they sat and talked about what had happened to Prince Gregory and the plan to rescue him from Nomans Land. The rescue, they knew, would not be an easy task, and Sir Anthony had many things to learn from Yoriah, the ancient one.

And when this was done, Sir Anthony took his rest, and in the morning when Sir Anthony was rested, he and Yoriah made further plans to save Prince Gregory from the evil dragons of Nomans Land. Then, after the plans were made and gone over, Yoriah

went into his stable and fetched his strongest and fastest horse. It was a very grand and beautiful white stallion with powerful shoulder muscles that rippled in the sunlight and a long flowing mane that gave testimony to the speed and strength of the horse. Then the magic man, Yoriah, brought forth the Star Crystal he had found that day while fetching water for his tea. Yoriah then told the young warrior, Sir Anthony, about the Star Crystal he had found. "This crystal I found," said Yoriah, "has many powers and will give you the power you need to reach Nomans Land." Then, without another word, Yoriah took the Star Stone Crystal and placed it on the forehead of

7

the great white stallion, and instantly the horse was magically transformed into a mighty and majestic Pegasus.

Sir Anthony was amazed at what he had just seen. Yoriah just smiled at the young warrior and said, "This, Sir Anthony, is my best work of all. You see, this Pegasus is the most powerful and fastest creature on earth. He will fly you to the stars and back again in a blink of an eye, and with his mighty wings you shall soar to Nomans Land and rescue your father from the evil dragons that took him there."

Chapter 2
Part 2

Shadow Land

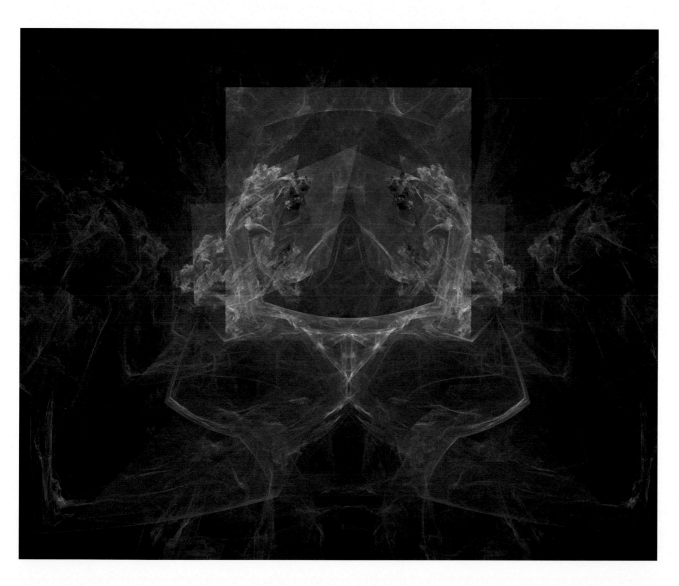

Sir Anthony was very grateful for what the magic man, Yoriah, had done for him, and now he knew that nothing could stand in his way in reaching Nomans Land. So Yoriah and the young warrior saddled and bridled the majestic Pegasus, and when they were done Sir Anthony mounted the mighty winged horse. It was then that Yoriah handed over the Star Stone Crystal to Sir Anthony and said to him, "You must use this Star Crystal to defeat the dragons of Nomans Land and destroy the Lord of Shadows. Take heart, my young warrior, for the time is at hand when you must rid the fair city of Goodinia from the evil dragons that descend upon it and free this land once and for all. For your father's very life depends upon you now, as well as Goodinia. Take heart, dear boy, for the Star Stone Crystal will show you the way. Follow your heart, Sir Anthony," said Yoriah, "and you shall prevail."

And with those words the mighty warrior, with the power of the Star Crystal and the love for his mother and father, turned the mighty Pegasus in the direction of Nomans Land. With the command and a mighty sweep from the wings of Pegasus, Sir Anthony was airborne and rising high above the clouds in flight as fast as a shooting star on his way to Nomans Land. Just before they were out of sight Yoriah smiled to himself and said, "Let the Star Stone Crystal show you the way. Make me proud, boy, and Godspeed to you, Sir Anthony."

Now Sir Anthony was making very good time and flying fast on the wings of Pegasus, the clouds rushing by underneath him. Looking down through the breaks between the clouds Sir Anthony could see land below. He could see hillsides and many mountains as he passed over them from above the clouds, and just ahead, though still very far away, he could see his destination in sight. Sir Anthony gave the command for Pegasus to pick up speed, and faster they flew, with the wind whipping by, blowing the young warrior's long blond hair. This made Sir Anthony feel as free as an eagle and also gave him a feeling of great power and strength he had never felt before. But all the while with these thoughts running through his mind he still could not stop thinking about how he was going to save his father and kill the dragon that took him and put an end to the terror from Nomans Land. Hours had passed now, and Sir Anthony had already flown halfway around the world and into the night sky. Flying at this altitude Sir Anthony could see the stars in the night and how brightly they shone, but with the speed at which they were flying the stars seemed to look as though they were shooting by at great speeds. Then suddenly, Sir Anthony shouted, "There it is: Nomans Land. Take us down, Pegasus."

So Pegasus began to descend to Nomans Land, and Sir Anthony was in luck, because with it being night and very dark the evil dragons would not be aware of Sir Anthony's

arrival. Now Pegasus flew further down, for the young warrior could see the cave where the dragons must be holding his father captive, because the cave was very heavily guarded by the evil dragons.

Sir Anthony told Pegasus to fly to the top of the cliff and land there, and the mighty Pegasus did what Sir Anthony said, and when they had landed, the young warrior, Sir Anthony, took from his pouch the Star Stone Crystal that Yoriah had given him. Because Sir Anthony was of royalty and pure of heart the Star Crystal gave to Sir Anthony all of its power, and the young warrior was now more powerful than a hundred men and felt new strength surge though his body, and he knew that all he had to do now was to go through the entrance of the cave and save his father. Sir Anthony was now unstoppable; no dragon was going to get in the way of his rescuing his father. This he knew. With this newfound strength that the Star Stone Crystal had given him, Sir Anthony gave the order to fly. Into the cave they flew, and just as Sir Anthony had suspected, there toward the back wall of the cave was his father, Prince Gregory. The evil dragons that had guarded the cave entrance were now surrounding him. Sir Anthony and Pegasus had made it just in time, for the dragons were about to roast Prince Gregory with their fiery breath.

"Stop, you evil dragons!" shouted Sir Anthony. "Father, are you all right?" asked the young warrior, and his father answered, "Yes, Anthony, but not for long. Did you bring help, son?"

And Sir Anthony shouted back, "Yes, Father, now take cover. I do not want you to get hurt in the attack." And with those words Prince Gregory took cover behind some rocks. Then Sir Anthony raised in his hand the Star Stone Crystal and aimed it at the evil dragons, for the Star Stone Crystal seemed to be telling Sir Anthony what to do. All of a sudden the crystal became a very bright glowing green and with great force began to shoot out great fireballs at the dragons, killing them in their tracks where they stood, and one by one the dragons, as evil as they were, fell to the ground. The noise was deafening, and then after the noise had faded away Prince Gregory shouted out, "By the powers that be, what was that?" He asked his son, "How did you slay all these dragons?"

Sir Anthony answered him, saying, "Don't you know, Father, that in order to kill a dragon you must fight fire with fire?"

"And so you have, my son, and so you have," said Prince Gregory. "Now let us get out of this cave and go home. After all, there could be more of them here, wouldn't you say, son?"

"Yes, Father," said Anthony. "But first I must destroy the Lord of Shadows."

"You are quite right, my son," said Prince Gregory, "and I shall help you."

Now Prince Gregory had never seen Pegasus before, but when Sir Anthony had climbed into the saddle his father did not ask any questions. He just followed his son and climbed on too and sat in the saddle behind Sir Anthony.

"Can this thing get us out of here?" asked his father, and Sir Anthony replied. "Hold onto me tight, Father. You are not going to believe this."

Sir Anthony chuckled, "Ha, ha, ha," and gave the command for Pegasus to take flight. Then suddenly, with darting speed, Pegasus took flight and with its mighty wings flew them out of the cave. And like a shooting star they were once again above the clouds with

the mighty wings of the great Pegasus thundering through the sky. Higher and higher they climbed as Pegasus began bolting through the sky like lightning on their way to defeat the Lord of Shadows and free the land of Goodinia forever from the forces of darkness and evil.

Just as Yoriah had promised Sir Anthony, the Star Stone Crystal did indeed lead the way, for it somehow told the mighty Pegasus where to fly. Now they were entering the realm of the Lord of Shadows, and in this realm, nothing Sir Anthony or his father could see had any solid substance; everything was shadowy and ghost-like, and Sir Anthony could feel the evil they had flown into.

"Look, Father, down there. What is that through the mist?" asked Sir Anthony as he pointed down into the mist.

"I don't know," said his father.

"It looks like two blazing eyes staring at us," said Prince Gregory.

Just then, the mighty Pegasus let out a loud noise, and Sir Anthony thought that Pegasus was somehow hurt by the pair of eyes. So Sir Anthony took out the Star Stone Crystal once again in hopes of healing Pegasus. But Pegasus was not hurt at all, for the noise that Pegasus made seemed to trigger some power within the Star Stone Crystal, and then the Star Stone Crystal began to glow again, only this time instead of green it began to become very yellow and as bright as the sun. So bright it was that it gave light down into Shadow Land. Then things became visible for Sir Anthony and Prince Gregory to see.

Now as Pegasus flew down into the land of the Lord of Shadows those blazing eyes that they had seen on the way in began to follow them, it seemed. This did not feel right to Sir Anthony, and because of the power he got from the Star Stone Crystal, wisdom told the young warrior that those eyes were the eyes of the Lord of Shadows himself. Then very quickly Sir Anthony told Pegasus to circle around and come in behind the Lord of Shadows so that they could take the upper hand to destroy this monster, and just as he was told, the mighty Pegasus circled back around and came in behind the Lord of Shadows. Then Sir Anthony took out his Star Crystal and held it out in front of him and began to have an idea, a great idea, for Sir Anthony knew what to do now—he began to use his wisdom. Then he held the Crystal in the palm of his hand, and chanted, "Enter the light by the power of the Star Crystal; darkness be gone." Sir Anthony continued to chant this, and suddenly the sky above him started to open up and light began to show through the dark mist, and thunder sounded in the sky. BOOM! BOOM! BOOM! went the thunder, and all the while the Star Stone Crystal began to get even brighter. Then it started a humming sound, and then with a loud crack the sky brought forth a huge hole, and as the Star Crystal started to rise off of Sir Anthony's hand and ascend up into the sky so did the Lord of Shadows get sucked up through the hole in the sky that the Star Crystal had created. Then when the Lord of Shadows was gone and out of sight, through the hole in the sky went all of Shadow Land, and all of the shadows and evil went with the evil Lord of Shadows. Then the sky sealed and closed up again, and the Lord of Shadows was destroyed and gone forever.

And then the most wonderful thing happened, there in what was Shadow Land, for a great rainbow appeared and covered over the land, and light filled the sky. Flowers began to spring up everywhere, and the land became so beautiful, for Sir Anthony had done what he had set out to do. He had saved his father and killed the evil dragons of Nomans Land and destroyed the Lord of Shadows. Now the city, his home, in Goodinia, would be safe once again.

And now Sir Anthony, his father Prince Gregory, and Pegasus, with nothing left to do but turn and head back home, did just that. They were above the clouds again, and every so often Pegasus would take them through the clouds so that they could see the land below them and then fly above the clouds again to gain speed. Sir Anthony was in a hurry to

reunite his father and mother, because he knew that his mother, Princess Patricia, must be worried sick with grief about him and his father, for they had been gone a few days now, without a word to her about their safety. But still, there was one stop that Sir Anthony had to make along the way, and Pegasus seemed to know what Sir Anthony was thinking, for the mighty Pegasus was already heading on his way back to the mountain of Yoriah.

Now flying faster than an eagle, Sir Anthony and Prince Gregory could see the mountain just ahead of them, and they were coming upon the mountain peak toward the castle of

Yoriah, so close now that they could see the rainbow above the great waterfall. The young warrior told Pegasus to take them down and land by the castle, and Pegasus did as Sir Anthony told him. When they touched the ground, Yoriah was already standing outside, waiting for them, for the eagle had told him of their arrival. Sir Anthony dismounted Pegasus first and then helped his father to dismount. Then Yoriah welcomed them back again and said to them, "Let us go into my castle and have tea together." So they did, for they had a lot to talk about. You see, not only was Yoriah a friend to the king and queen of Goodinia, but he was also Prince Gregory's grandfather and a great-grandfather to Sir Anthony.

Chapter 3

Part 3

The Journey Home

Once inside the castle Prince Gregory was astonished by what he saw. The walls of the grand entryway leading to the dining hall were filled with many paintings of the king and queen of Goodinia, and further along were paintings of Gregory and Patricia, the prince and princess of Goodinia, and also paintings of Sir Anthony when he just a little boy in the arms of his mother, Princess Patricia. Sir Anthony was very proud to see all these paintings of his family, but he was very confused as to why Yoriah had these paintings, and so he asked Yoriah why he kept such paintings of him and his family. With a warm smile Yoriah said to him, "Have you not been told, my son, that I am your great-grandfather?"

"Why no!" said Sir Anthony, "but I am very happy that you are, for now you can teach me many things and I can learn from you great and wondrous magic and wisdom. Will you teach me these things, Great-grandfather?" asked Sir Anthony.

Yoriah was very happy and honored by what Sir Anthony had asked of him, but it was with great joy and at the same time great sorrow that Yoriah said to the young warrior, "My dear boy, you must learn these things from your mother and father, for they alone must teach you all the things you ask of me. They will teach you, and from their wisdom you shall learn and become a great leader of men, and one day you shall rule over the great land of Goodinia. For it is written that a very young and mighty warrior shall rise up from the land and set free the land and destroy the evil dragons of Nomans Land and put an end to the evil Lord of Shadows forever. And this mighty warrior shall be named king one day and reign over the land of Goodinia."

Then Yoriah said this prophecy, "Sir Anthony, this was written a long time ago, and now the prophecy has been fulfilled. This prophecy was of you, Sir Anthony, for you shall become king."

Just then, Sir Anthony turned to his father, Prince Gregory, and as the young warrior looked at his father he saw tears running down his cheeks.

"Why are you crying, Father?" asked Sir Anthony, and his father said to him, "Son, I am very proud of you. I love you so much; you are very dear to my heart. You have saved your father's life, and you have defeated the dragons of Nomans Land and destroyed the Lord of Shadows. My son, Sir Anthony, you have fulfilled your prophesy and made me very proud of you, and the people of Goodinia will be very proud of you too for what you have done."

Then Sir Anthony said to his father, "Father, I love you."

And then Prince Gregory gave Sir Anthony a great big hug, and their hearts were filled with joy.

Seeing all this made Yoriah start to cry too. Tears were welling up in the magical man's eyes, and as Yoriah wiped away the tears from his eyes he said to Prince Gregory and Sir Anthony, "Come, let us go and have our tea now, for you both have a long journey ahead of you, and you must be refreshed."

So Yoriah, Prince Gregory, and Sir Anthony went into the dining hall to have their tea.

"This tea is very good," said Sir Anthony.

"Yes it is," said his father.

"You know," said Yoriah, "you cannot go on your journey without wings to take you there. So I want you to have Pegasus. He has taken a liking to you, Sir Anthony, and he has told me that he wants to stay with you."

"Oh! May I, Father? May I keep Pegasus?" Sir Anthony asked his father.

"Yes, you may," said Prince Gregory, "for Pegasus shall be quite useful to you when it is your time to become king."

"Oh! Thank you, Father," said Sir Anthony. It made Sir Anthony very happy to have his very own flying horse, and he could not wait to go home to tell his mother, Princess Patricia, what he had done and to tell her all about Yoriah and show her his new flying horse, Pegasus. The mighty warrior could not wait to see his mother again. He missed her very much.

Two hours had passed since they had sat down to have their tea, and they had talked about many things, but now it was time for Sir Anthony and Prince Gregory to fly home to Princess Patricia on the wings of Pegasus.

So they gathered fresh supplies for their trip home, and Sir Anthony made a special effort to gather plenty of tea, for he liked the tea Yoriah had made very much; it was very good. Then they all said their goodbyes, and Sir Anthony and his father saddled the mighty Pegasus once again. Just before the mighty Pegasus took to the air, Yoriah said to Sir Anthony, "Wait, I have something to give to you." Then he handed over to Sir Anthony the other piece of the Star Stone Crystal and said to him, "This Star Crystal will help you one day to serve as king. Take it." The young warrior did what Yoriah told him to do. Then, like a shot, the mighty Pegasus took to the air, and they were off and on their way home to Goodinia.

Back home in the land of Goodinia in the royal castle Princess Patricia was preparing dinner. She did not know that her husband and son were returning that day. She was doing what she had been doing for the past few days to keep from going completely insane with worry, for she loved to cook, and at this time she had a roast in the oven. The aroma of the roast smelled so good. Princess Patricia was after all a very fine cook, and she knew her way around the kitchen. She was baking a rye bread that she and her husband loved very much, and she had baked a butter bread that she knew Sir Anthony liked. Princess Patricia spent much of her time cooking and baking, for she found that doing this kept her from thinking ill thoughts of what might have happened to her husband and son. They had been gone now for quite a long time, and she did not know where they might be, and she had not heard any news about them, and she did not know that she would be surprised by their return this day. So she stayed busy cooking.

The roast was now done, and she took it from the oven and set it on the table. Then she took the breads out of the oven, for they were done too, and she placed the breads on the table next to the roast.

"Hmmmm! Dinner smells very good," said Patricia. "Now I must get these cakes in the oven, a cherry cake and a chocolate cake." For they were her favorites, and Princess Patricia made them so very delicious too.

Princess Patricia was a lady of many talents. She had a voice like that of a songbird, and she loved to sing and tell stories to her son, Sir Anthony. Oh how she wished that her son and husband were home now! She missed them so much, and she prayed every night since they'd been gone for their safe return home. Princess Patricia could not bear to think about what her life might be like without them. Just then, the bell to the oven sounded, telling her that her cakes were done. So she took them out of the oven and placed them on the table to cool so she could ice them. Oh how good they smelled too!

"Yum! Yum! Yum!" she said.

Princess Patricia decided she would go and take a warm soothing bath while her cakes were cooling down.

"How I wish my husband and son would come home today. I miss them so much," said the princess, and then she turned on the water to let her bathtub fill up. She got into the tub and had her bath and then got out of the tub and dried herself off. She entered her dressing room and was getting dressed in her finest gown. She had picked out her most favorite gown of all; it was a blue one, a magnificent color with white lace and trim. She put it on, and Patricia was so beautiful in her dress. She walked over to her dressing room window and opened it up to let in some fresh air. She enjoyed looking out over the cliffs of Goodinia, for she had a perfect view of the ocean from her window. She could see the waves on the ocean as they splashed against the rocks and could smell the salty mist rising from the waves as they crashed against the rocks.

Princess Patricia loved this land she lived in, and looking out her window she could see, as far as the eye could see, the countryside, forests, and mountains. How beautiful these things were to her. It was a fine day in the land of Goodinia. The sun was shining.

The sky was so blue, with puffy white clouds, and birds were chirping and singing to one another. This made Princess Patricia smile, and she could not get over how beautiful the sky looked to her. She had the feeling that this day was somehow very special, and as she gazed up into the clouds she saw something very far away, but she couldn't quite make out what it was. So she kept watching, and as it got closer it began to get bigger. Just then, Princess Patricia felt her heart jump, because she realized that what she was seeing was a very giant flying bird. At least she thought it was a bird, for it had wings, but then as it got steadily closer she was amazed at what she actually saw. Then tears began to flow from the princess's eyes, and she could not stop crying, for she was so happy. She raised her arm and began to wave, because Princess Patricia finally saw what she had been praying for, for the past few days and nights.

"Thank heaven," shouted the princess. She was so happy. Her husband, Prince Gregory, and her son, Sir Anthony, had returned home to her. She could not wait to have her family in her arms again, so she quickly closed her window and started to run out her dressing room and down the hall. Then down the stairs she flew, and she was out the door just as the mighty Pegasus landed. Prince Gregory and Sir Anthony jumped down out of the saddle, and with tears still in Princess Patricia's eyes she ran to her husband. Prince Gregory swept her off her feet and said to his beloved wife, "I love you more than words could ever say."

"I love you too, Gregory," said the princess, and then she gave her son, Sir Anthony, the biggest hug, and she kissed his forehead and said, "Oh son, you have made your mother so happy. I am so glad you've come home with your father. I am so happy." Tears fell from her eyes, and then she was laughing with joy as she asked, "What is this you flew in on? I've never seen a horse with wings before. What is this creature?"

"Why, it is my Pegasus," said Anthony "Isn't he pretty?" Then he added, "Yoriah gave him to me, and Daddy said I could keep him."

Then Princess Patricia looked to her husband, and Prince Gregory said, "It's a long story, and we have much to talk about."

Then they all three, and even Pegasus, began to laugh, and this made Patricia laugh all the more. Then the princess said to her husband and son, "Come into the castle with me, my loves. I have made dinner, and it just so happens that I have made you your favorite cakes. You must be hungry after what you have been through."

"Oh yes, we are!" they shouted at once.

So Princess Patricia, Prince Gregory, and Sir Anthony went inside their castle and lived happily ever after. So ends this journey of Sir Anthony and the Star Stone Crystal. Until we meet again on our next journey.

Printed in the United States
by Baker & Taylor Publisher Services